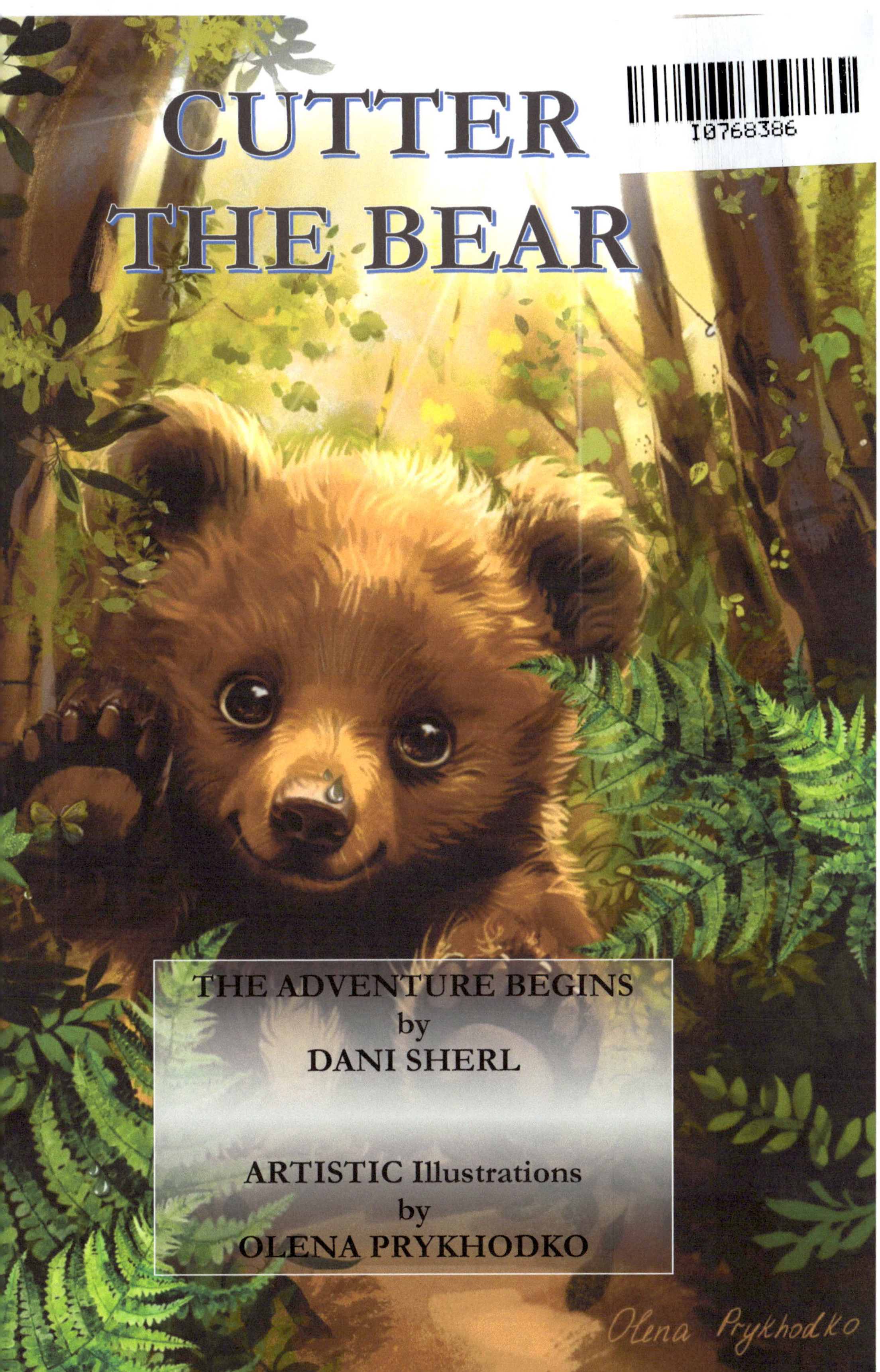

CUTTER THE BEAR
THE ADVENTURE BEGINS
by
DANI SHERL

ARTISTIC Illustrations
by
OLENA PRYKHODKO

CUTTER THE BEAR

Paperback ISBN: 978-1-969775-71-0
LCCN: 2025918584

DEDICATION

Lovingly dedicated to David Louis, my friend and son, MaryAnn, our daughter in love, and Oliver Luke my grandson

Originally written - March 22, 1990

CONTENTS

ACKNOWLEDGMENTS

No book is published without extensive work by important people. I would like to acknowledge several here. First is my wife and love of my life, the mother of our son and grandmother of our grandchild. Also, for her being able to put up with me all these years.

The contributors to this book include design artist Olena Prykhodko that provided the wonderful characterizations of the forest and farm animals. Her background, experience and talents are phenomenal.

Thanks to Debora Wondercheck, Founder and CEO of the Arts & Learning Institute for her guidance and involvement in working with young artists and entertainers.

And, thanks to Jim Waynes, Jay Cooper, PhD and Nathan Clark of the Book Publishing Professionals for making this book series possible.

As in the story, wonderful things can be achieved through working together and appreciating each person's talents.

Olena Prykhodko

CUTTER

The morning dew fell from the soft, green fern leaf like a small, clear pea bursting on the tip of Cutter's coarse, black nose. He snorted, then pushed the pine needles of his bed around as the next drop ended his deep sleep with a startle.

As he rubbed the sleep from his big, brown eyes with paws as big as a house cat, he thought, "What a wonderful day to be alive!" The chirping of the family of birds living in the nearby birch tree tickled his ears as he stood up, stretched, and sniffed the air to see what adventure awaited him today.

With a sparkle in his eye, he bounded for his mom and dad's bed. With a bump, he landed between them. Dad grumbled, and Mom groaned while Cutter pushed, nuzzled, and licked their furry cheeks.

"Ok, ok," Dad said as he and Cutter tumbled from the soft pine bed. "You're getting bigger and smarter every day."

Cutter was getting bigger; he was almost a year old—no longer a baby, and he knew it. When he stood up, he was taller than most of his friends who weren't bears, even though they were a little older. He was small for a bear, though, but he knew he would be one of the best there was. Just like his dad.

"Mom, I like our house!"

"That's nice Cutter", she replied. "It's a den", she added. "A den?" Cutter asked. "Yes, bears live in dens. They are usually in caves like this. We find a cave, move out stuff we don't want and move in what we need. Look around!" she continued.

And, he saw it. His warm bed of pine branches on soft needles, the area of packed dirt that they all sat on to eat the food Dad brought back as well as Mom and Dad's bed. It was all surrounded by the cave walls made of rocks, stones and mud with scratches from carving out spaces made for exercise or just to relieve frustration. It was a warm and happy place.

"Let's eat breakfast, get cleaned up, and begin a new day," Dad said as he scooped Cutter up and went off toward the nearby stream.

It was going to be another day of adventure, indeed.

SOPHIE

"Geese are incredible!" Cutter's dad said. "They look elegant with their long necks, blue eyes edged with orange that match their beaks, and webbed feet.

"On farms and with other animals, they act as guards. Bother some of the smallest animals, and you will hear them approaching, honking with their beaks open to defend the smallest ones. Dinner's ready.

"Have fun! I'm going back home," Cutter's dad said as he turned and walked away.

Sophie was amazing. She was fun to talk with, played great games, and laughed a lot—and loudly. She was an adventurer. Her big, blue eyes took in everything.

The bright blue sky with floating clouds was part of her life. And she could fly high if she wanted to. But she preferred to stay on the ground with her friends and the opportunities it afforded her.

Sophie could hear the slightest sound and literally taste the air through her narcs.

"You can taste it, can't you?" Sophie said, with a honk. "Taste what? You haven't put anything in your mouth," Cutter replied.

"With your narcs, like mine," she smiled and said.

"What's a narc?" asked Cutter.

"I told you that. You have them too! Two holes in your nose. Mine are just on my beak," Sophie calmly replied.

"You remember that?" he asked.

"I remember everything, and don't you forget it," she reminded him as they walked down the path to the stream.

Sophie was indeed up for an adventure. Neither of them knew how close it was and how soon it would come.

Olena Prykhodko

MISSING

The tall green grass lined the path most of them took from the forest and the farm to the stream and pond. In the summer, it was warm, sunny, and had the feel of wrapping yourself in a blanket or towel after a swim.

The path was one originally made by the forest animals but was now also used by humans and farm animals. The grass was first laid down by getting stepped on, then gradually disappeared as the soil muddied, then hardened.

The hardened path then became two as farmers, campers, and others started using small vehicles on it to move themselves and the things they needed around.

The animals liked it and also feared some parts. The path took them where they wanted to go, but it also was a potential trap, exposing them to predators. It was nice to travel, but they knew to be alert.

Some kept to the sides near the grasses and shrub brush, jumping quickly and quietly if something alerted them. Others simply froze and didn't move until the area seemed safe. And some would find peril freezing in place when a light at night was shone on them. The light sometimes was the headlight of a vehicle, and the driver wouldn't see the animal until it was too late.

Farm animals met their forest friends almost every day. They played, wrestled, and talked.

The humans on the farm and the hikers, campers, and hunters in the forest didn't recognize the languages or realize that all the others knew what each one was saying.

So, when Carlos told Cutter and Sophie that Ancho was missing, they all became very alert. Then, they heard it.

At first, it was muffled, but Cutter said it was Ancho in pain.

Did the farmer do this? Ancho was a young small chicken. She told them about feeling that she would soon lay eggs.

"What do we do?" cried Carlos. "Do we get your dad, Cutter? Do we make a fuss with the farmer? Do we get closer? Or do we just wait and see?"

Cutter looked at Sophie. She simply said, "I know you, Cutter, and I know you know what to do."

Cutter replied, "We must all do this together. We'll follow the sounds, smells, and things we see and feel as we get closer. But watch for Amrac, Nella, the hunters, and the farmers. They all know we use the path."

CARLOS

Waking up on the front porch of the farmhouse was always Carlos' favorite time. Shaking off the nighttime dust from his golden fur got his energy going. He automatically knew that his food and water dishes were freshly filled by his "master."

Master, he thought with a smile. The relationship was more of a mutual trust. He felt loved and appreciated. In return, he would play games, chase other animals, and bark at strangers or danger. His animal friends knew that his chasing them was a game. They laughed and sometimes said they had enough of his silliness.

His mom and dad were from a different farm, but he especially remembered his mom and her loving snuggle and wonderful milk.

He wanted to be like his dad, who was more of a hunter, greatly admired by other farmers and the most beautiful of golden retrievers. He was "purebred," whatever that meant.

The porch, like the rest of the farmhouse, was simply made of wood, unpainted and weathered over the twenty-some years that it was home to the farmer, his family, and farm animals.

It was wide enough to fit a hanging swing, made of wood painted white, built as a kind of wide chair that could hold three people or a beautiful dog and a cat together. A chain on each side held the swing, enabling it to move back and forth or gently move as its occupants relaxed in the shade of the wooden roof.

Pigeons moved into the spaces above the wooden beams holding the roof and had their families, cooing on the best of days.

For Carlos, this morning's wake-up was different. He loved Ancho. She was the first he would see every day as she strutted, clucked, and pecked at the wooden porch floor in front of him.

She was beautiful, with a bright red comb, clean brown feathers, and young and energetic.

"Why not today?" he thought. "Where could she be? I have to find her!"

THE TRAIL

Following a trail is different from going down a path. A trail consists of clues—things that show you that something or someone you are looking for came through an area. It could be a path, road, or another thing that gives you that clue. That includes paw prints in the mud, brush or grasses disturbed by being moved, even small pieces of fur, feathers, or scales on the ground or stuck to a bush.

Trail following has the added risk of following so closely that you don't notice something that could harm you.

Finding Cutter and Sophie at the edge of the farm gave Carlos a sense of relief. He felt a little better searching with them. They were friends, and they trusted each other.

He especially loved the abilities they each had. Cutter was smart, his hearing was on par with Carlos', and his sense of smell was great. Sophie could see things that everyone else missed. She was super protective of all of the other animals on the farm and the forest too.

But Ancho was still missing. Carlos trusted his farmer but not the hunters—or the others. That meant other farmers, campers, and large farm animals such as bulls, cows, and pigs that could step or fall on her by accident.

And then there were the forest animals like Amrac and Nella. Both of them lived off animals that were hurt, dying, or stuck somewhere.

Each of them had their part of the forest and sometimes the farm as their domain. When hungry enough, anything was possible with them. They constantly watched the trail from their individual hiding places.

Amrac was always quick to say, "Everywhere and everything is mine for the taking if I want!"

Nella's eyes always glistened as she watched for those she called "prey."

AMRAC

"Amrac is a wolf?" Sophie asked.

"What is a wolf? My heritage includes wolves, so am I also a wolf?" Carlos asked as they began to walk down the trail. They all shook their heads, "no," as Sophie explained that wolves live in forests and dogs are usually happy with all others, including those called humans.

"Each of us has an area that we really get to love. We get to know where and what to eat, who to trust, and what others want and need," she further explained.

Amrac uses his hyper senses to find food, a place to live, sleep, and relax when he wanted. He was born to a pack years ago. His father taught him how to find food, how to capture it, and what to do next.

He missed that, but he now saw something different coming his way. "Who are they, and what do they want? Maybe better yet, what do they taste like?" his brain thought.

A bear, a dog, and a goose? They had gotten off the path and were following some kind of trail. What were they looking for? Why were they coming into his domain? "Let's just watch and see," he fed back into his brain.

He listened as they got closer. They were telling each other their stories—who they were, what they could do, and how they wanted to find something.

"Now is the time!" his brain shouted, as it usually did to get him something.

THE WOLF

"I'll tell you my story!"

Everyone froze. The voice was booming. Fur and feathers rose on their necks, and their eyes grew big, searching both sides of the trail. Cutter's ears could hear leaves falling to the ground. Birds in the trees chirped rapidly, then suddenly stopped.

Carlos could feel his heart beating in his chest, his eyes narrowing, and his teeth beginning to show between his lips, parted in a sneer.

"But you might not want to hear it!" Again, a loud command.

"We're listening!" Sophie said in an even tone while her body lowered to the ground, her neck lowered, and her beak widened as her head focused through the slits of her eyes. Everyone knew this was the farm guardian, ready for an intruder meaning to harm her friends.

"First, tell me what such a focused group is doing in my domain!"

"Your domain?" Cutter shouted, startling himself.

"Do you want to talk or fight?" Amrac replied in a calmer voice. "I'm not telling you anything until I know what you are obviously looking for."

Sophie's 360-degree vision, because of her eyes on different sides of her head, found him on the left side of the trail, almost completely camouflaged.

He was a beautiful animal with a fur coat laced with white, gray, and black. His eyes were an intense blue. He wasn't snarling or looking like he was about to pounce.

"We're looking for our friend. We lost her today and heard her cry out, so we're here to help her," Sophie replied as she changed her posture by standing taller, widening her eyes, and closing her attack beak. "You can come out now if you want to talk."

The brush and bushes moved gently and slowly as Amrac pushed through them with his nose and face. The green grass, over a foot tall, parted like the curtain on a theater stage as the main character came out.

He walked out, slowly and purposely, but not threateningly.

NELLA

After he heard the story of Ancho, Amrac the wolf said, "I know this area and those that come here, including you, Cutter. I know your father and mother and respect both of them."

Cutter replied, "Then it is you that my father talked about. It was also with respect."

"He said that you were originally from another forest, high in the mountains, and that you came here for a better life, just like him," said Cutter.

"Tell us your story!" said Carlos. "Tell us while we walk. Tell us where you think Ancho could be and who could be involved."

"First, as we go, I want all of you to be alert for Nella as well as hunters and campers. We'll also pass another farm. The farmer and their hands, as they call the others, are very cruel to those of us on their farm, including their dog, cat, and other farm animals," Amrac finished.

"Tell us about Nella," asked Sophie.

"First, let me tell you about me. Nella can tell you what she wants you to know when you meet her. Be aware that she is venomous and very hard to see until it is too late."

Just then, Cutter heard the faint rustle of leaves and grass, but it stopped. He tuned in his hearing and carefully looked at the grass and shrubs near them. He saw and heard nothing.

"Your father and I came from almost opposite directions. Your father got here, met your mother, and they decided to build a family here. My family was destroyed by hunters. They talked about how we wolves were a danger to the animals they hunted and to themselves, so they went out to kill us all.

"I was very young when my mother was caught in a steel trap and my father was shot trying to get her out. I was there, and my father pointed and said, 'Go now! Don't stop until it is very far and very safe!'" It was terrifying, but I did what I was told and later knew it was the reason that I am still alive.

THE JOURNEY

"You two get along just fine because a bear and a wolf are almost the same!" said Carlos.

"A little while ago, you said that a wolf was the same as you, a dog," added Sophie. "Aren't we all the same in a larger respect? We're all living creatures. We're proving it here by searching for Ancho, someone that many would say is worlds different from the rest of us."

"We're not the same, Amrac!" replied Cutter. "You hunt the rest of us just to feed yourself. That's not me!"

"Really? I told you I know you because I know the forest. Don't you go to the stream and catch fish to eat?" Amrac asked calmly.

Cutter calmed and replied, "Ok. Let's focus. We need to find her as fast as possible, especially if she is hurt or in danger of being killed. Sophie, can you and Amrac work together on a plan?"

Sophie replied, "Love to!" energetically with a cackle.

"Me too!" Amrac agreed.

The forest was quiet and calm. The trees overhead gave great shade to the green bushes and tall, green grass below. If you listened closely, you could hear the birds chirping and singing while gathering nuts and berries, and going back and forth to their nests.

"Stop!" shouted Cutter. "Don't step!"

They froze as the grass alongside them on the right moved slowly. Motionless, they all heard the hiss.

"Nella! I knew you were here. How long have you been following us?" asked Amrac.

"Longer than any of you can imagine," Nella replied with a hiss. "I've heard all of your stories from the time that Carlos told you about Ancho, the chicken."

"If you are venomous and we didn't know you were there, why haven't you bitten all or even one of us?" asked Sophie.

"Now, how would that be a challenge? Where would the excitement be? Besides, I'm interested in finding Ancho, and not for the reason you think."

"Why?" they all responded together.

"Because I'm not who you think I am," answered Nella.

TOGETHER

"Ever hear anybody say 'snake' and happily point to the snake?" Nella began. They all looked at each other with surprised expressions—some thinking, some smiling, and Cutter laughing knowingly.

"I've heard each of your stories, and that is the best reason for me to want to join you. So, here's mine as we go forward," Nella said softly.

"Wait!" Sophie honked while raising her long white feathered wing. "Before we go too much farther, we have to plan how we pass the farm coming up, the hunters near the pond, and the campers we may come across. As a group, we would get a lot of attention, all for the wrong reasons," guided Sophie. "We all have our individual strengths as well as weaknesses that the others make better. I just described the threats that we all know. Our mission is to use the opportunities to find, help, or save Ancho."

"First, the farm," said Cutter.

"The workers were fixing the fence near the path this morning. They cleared a lot of grasses, some trees, and bushes," Amrac whispered.

"I'll take a quick look," Nella replied and quietly moved into the grass along the left side of the path. The next thing they knew, she was back.

"They're back at the barn milking the cows, so we can go quickly. I didn't see Ancho or anything that looked like she could have been caught or harmed," Nella said with her standard hiss.

"I have to run back to my farmhouse. It's about the time that my farmer feeds me. If I'm not there, he will come looking and calling for me. I can catch up with you closer to the pond," Carlos said as he ran back down the path.

"We'll miss him, but we can work together, and he will join up on the other side of this farm," Cutter quietly said.

The walk was quick, and this time Amrac, the wolf and Nella the snake went down the path first, with Nella on the uncut grass on the left. Amrac heard multiple growls. While back at the the rest of the group, Cutter heard it first, and they all stopped and crouched down at his paw signal.

"Come to join us now?" growled the largest of two wolves. The other stayed on the left side, baring its teeth in an angry threat.

"I told you before. I'm a lone wolf," emphasizing the word "lone" loudly, replied Amrac.

"That's not what I heard from the birds. They said you were with a strange group that even included a goose and a snake."

"A venomous snake," calmly interrupted Amrac as the grass and brush near the other wolf suddenly moved, causing both wolves to jump away quickly.

"We know who you are looking for and haven't seen Ancho," the other wolf quietly said.

"If you know that, do you know what happened to her and where she is?" asked Sophie as she waddled up next to Amrac with her neck, back, and head low and her low-pitched honk. Cutter stood next to Sophie with his eyes narrow, his teeth showing, and his body revealing his young muscles.

"I've seen her with the campers near the pond," said the big wolf. "They have a rope around her neck. One of them said it was to keep her from getting lost again."

Just then, running footsteps and a loud bark signaled the arrival of Carlos. He stopped with a tumble that was his classic way of ending his fastest run.

Cutter smiled and said, "It's okay." As Carlos relaxed, both wolves, Sophie, and Cutter all eased up.

"We'd help if we could," said the large wolf. "But three wolves, a bear, and a snake—if they see her—would make the campers do something because they were scared. We'll stay here and make sure the path is clear for you to get back."

He wasn't even done talking when Cutter noticed the sound of the grass moving quickly and the soft hiss as Nella moved like a bolt of lightning.

Carlos started to run when Sophie blocked him and said, "We need a plan if no one is to get hurt." So, they waved "thank you" to the wolves and began to move quickly down the path. The stream was great because it babbled noisily, hiding any sounds they were making.

Then they saw the campground with a single tent, a small fire surrounded by rocks, and a water pot hanging over it. There were two campers—a man and a woman—sitting near the fire, drinking something that looked hot with steam rising from the tops. A little farther away, they saw Ancho sitting quietly, looking the other way. She had a rope around her neck but didn't look hurt or injured.

"I wonder where she came from?" they heard the woman say to the man.

"I'd hate to see her hurt or worse," replied the man.

"I could slither in, then hiss and show them my fangs," said Nella as they all jumped at her unexpected sudden appearance.

"No. I'll go get her. She knows me and is my best friend," said Carlos as he again began to go toward the tent.

"Here's the plan," said Sophie, again blocking Carlos.

Before he could push her away, Sophie continued, "Yes, you are to go in. Ancho will see you first and cluck happily. Go straight to her. Nuzzle her like I know you want to do desperately.

"The campers will try to catch you as you go to her. That's when we help.

"We start by making noises in the forest around them. They will watch us and be scared. You will make them see you go quickly and nuzzle Ancho.

"Then you will turn and get between the campers and us and growl, bark, and show your teeth at us, turning a few times at them, smiling, and wagging your tail.

"After that, turn to us and charge, barking. We will all noisily run away. You go back, wagging your tail. Right before you reach them, you turn to the trail and get them to follow you back to the farm.

"We'll stay in the brush and release Ancho when they follow you. Agreed?"

They all nodded their heads.

It went exactly as Sophie planned, with one exception.

The lady turned, picked up Ancho, and told the man, "Let's take her back with us to where this beautiful golden retriever lives. I bet they know where she belongs."

And so as the other animals kept out of sight, the campers, holding Ancho led by Carlos, walked back past the stream, the other farm, down the path to Carlos and Ancho's farmhouse. The farmer was sitting on the swing on the porch and heard them approach.

Carlos, Ancho, and every other animal had tears in their eyes as the farmer saw them and hugged the campers and his two friends on his front porch.

"An adventure indeed!" thought Cutter.

SUNSET

The porch was warm and friendly as it always was with Carlos and Ancho enjoying each other's company. This time, the campers sat on the swing, gently moving back and forth as the farmer warmly leaned against the front porch post. His checkered red and black shirt highlighted his brown and silver hair.

His grey beard was trimmed and the sides of his face shaved clean. His name was Marcus, he told the campers. They replied that they were Julie and Clement, or Clem as his friends called him. They explained that it was the first time they camped in this area. Finding Ancho, as the farmer let them know she was called, made this one of the best experiences they had enjoyed together.

"But", Clem said. "I saw a bear, a wolf and heard the faint hiss of a snake, when Carlos, great name, by the way, barked and protected us.

"If you come back again or stay long enough and pay attention, you will find a great bond between all the farm and forest animals" Marcus added as they enjoyed the table of snacks and drinks that he brought out.

"This is great! Thank you for your hospitality" Julie said with a smile brightening her warm face. "What's really great is to have Carlos and Ancho back" Marcus replied as Carlos happily ate his dinner and Ancho pecked at her corn kernels on the wooden floor.

"I swore that I just saw the bushes move and what looked like the ears and eyes of a brown bear looking out at us" Clem said, pointing at moving brush. "Welcome to the world!" Marcus replied. "I've seen them all at various times".

"Do you think they know what we are saying?" Julie asked. "Sit!" commanded Marcus. Carlos sat up with his back straight, his ears turned toward them and his mouth, a big smile. "What do you think?" replied Marcus to Julie. She nodded.

"But, can you understand them?" she continued. "Where do you think I got the name for Ancho, a young, beautiful chicken." They all looked at Ancho and noticed that she was also sitting up straight next to Carlos, kind of looking like she was smiling.

They all heard the rustle of the brush, branches and grass as they saw glimpses of fur and feathers gently moving away.

The sun was setting with a warm glow. The pigeons returned to the nests in the porch rafters with classic cooing.

"An Adventure Indeed" again thought Cutter. "What's next for us?"

ABOUT THE AUTHOR

My mom had a typewriter. It wasn't fancy, as I recall, but it worked. I was intrigued by it, as well as the local newspaper that I was lucky enough to deliver. So, I began to type the news of our neighborhood, *The Patch*. I typed my first edition with headlines such as *Mrs. XXX Hangs Underwear on Her Clothesline (name withheld to prevent embarrassment)*.

After realizing that I had to retype everything for each new subscriber, I convinced my mom to take me to the drugstore to buy a dozen sheets of carbon paper. When we got home, she wanted to see what I was working on, thinking it was a school project. Needless to say, I learned about the censorship of the press.

But I also felt the impact of the craft of writing. Eventually, I became a publisher of magazines (or periodicals, if you prefer). I focused on building the business aspect of magazine publishing and was relatively successful. It provided a great and rewarding career.

However, I truly admired and appreciated the craftspeople who create great stories and information—whether through creative writing or the thoughtful compilation and assessment of past, present, and future knowledge and predictions.

~Dani Sherl

ABOUT THE ILLUSTRATOR

My mom's name is Olena Prykhodko, and I know how much heart she put into the drawings for this book. She's always been able to draw — she has an art education, and back in Ukraine, she used to create beautiful illustrations. I remember one of her drawings: a girl sitting right at the edge — maybe of a roof or a cliff — looking out into the distance. It felt like a dream captured on paper.

When I was little, my mom and I used to read picture books together. She would read them aloud, turn the pages, and show me the illustrations — magical and kind, just like the ones in this book, only in Russian or Ukrainian.

Then everything changed — we moved to Germany, and for a while, my mom stopped drawing. Later, we moved again — this time to America. That's when I saw her start drawing again, picking up pencils and paints like her inspiration had returned.

Now my mom works as an interior designer and decorator. She uses modern tools, even artificial intelligence. But when Dani asked her to illustrate this book, she came to life — her eyes lit up, as if the story had been living inside her all along. I even helped a little — I shared ideas and watched her drawings come to life.

I think my mom is happiest when she draws for children. There's warmth, magic, and love in her pictures. And I love being nearby when she's creating something new.

~By Yeva, the daughter of the Olena Prykhodko

KIMBER

This book was produced through long life experiences of animals, and the forest, farms and homes they enjoy with us.

This is the first in a series of ten books that focus on the love for the environment, those that live in it, their and our interactions while living together. Coming across others that are warm, threatening, dangerous or oblivious is part of life.

We're looking for those of you: young thinkers, talented, with a dream or vision of how this will grow. If you are a "KIMBER or want to be one, let us know. We're looking for writers and story tellers. I think it is a great way to grow and provide something that benefits us all.

KIMBER stands for "Kid In Mom's Basement Everyone Remembers" That's where I started.

If, you are one, let us know. If you enjoy the great outdoors, forests, farms, and animals, we love you.

We enjoy experiencing others environments, including deserts, lakes and streams, oceans, aquariums and zoos.

Enjoy the Book!

~Dan Charobee, Founder.

cutterthebear.com